LOVE ME Forever

Book Three Of The Bad Behavior Series

BY AWARD-WINNING AUTHOR
M.D. LABELLE

1

Chapter 1: The Call Of The Wild

I am rudely awakened in the middle of the night by the sound of Jon's voice as he shakes me while staring at me with wide eyes and demands, "Wake up. I want to show you something."

While I fight the urge to tell him to fuck off, I try to open my eyes fully and sit up as I stretch my sore muscles. We had outdone ourselves with the love making session and now as it appears, I won't be getting any more sleep either. "Oh well." I murmur under my breath as I scratch the back of my neck and scan the room.

By the time I realize it is only 4 a.m., I am already up and running. Not to mention, in the car with a cup of really strong black coffee. "Do you mind telling me what the hell is going on? All you have said so far is that you want to show me something and that I will really enjoy it. That does not give me much to go by now does it?" I state sarcastically as he starts up the car and then we head South on route 95.

"I know that I should say more, but just wait until we get there. I promise you will love it, or at least if you are anything like me you will. After all, you shared something with me, now it is my turn." He says mischievously as he winks at me with a lecherous grin.

I swallow hard before I turn to gaze out the window at the stars that are shining so brightly. They light our way to wherever we are going. As to where, I have absolutely no clue, and it is starting to scare me a little. I can already feel Joanna trying to take over as I struggle to keep her at bay.

For some reason, when he pulls into a stretch of wood unfamiliar to me, I am not surprised at all. Matter of fact, I find myself quite curious now, so I look over at him and cock my head before asking curiously, "So, now that we are here, do you care to tell me what we are doing here?"

He smirks and then cuts the engine before he laughs nervously and replies hesitantly, "I want to play a game. Shall we?"

"What kind of game?" I ask quietly while daring to stare eye to eye with him to see who will blink first.

"Why, a hunting game. Now, do I have your attention? Since we both have the same pass time, I thought I would see if I can catch you." He replies in amusement when I see that same old familiar mischievous glint appear in his eyes.

"Hm. Maybe. But what happens if you don't?" I say slowly while gauging his reaction.

"I don't want to spoil the surprise." He murmurs under his breath as the vein in his forehead starts to pulsate.

"Now, I will give you a small head start." He states as he motions for me to run.

When he raises his voice and yells, "You only have a minute to get ahead of me before I will hunt you down and then eat you." I swivel around on the heel of my snickers.

I run like the wind into the deep, dark woods as my primal instinct kicks in and the adrenaline rushes through my veins. As I keep a steady pace, I measure my breathing, so I don't get out of breath, and I focus on the path ahead of me. Not only am I in the greatest shape of my life, but I am younger than he is. So, that definitely gives me the advantage. However, when I hear him antagonize me by yelling at the top of his lungs, "I am coming to get you

Joanna." I feel this overwhelming sensation of dread and my heart beats up into my throat.

I don't know where it came from, but suddenly, I realize how my prey must feel when I slit their throat. That fear that drives you on enables me to move faster than ever before as I feel the power surge through every fiber of my being. "Now, how do I use this to my advantage?" I hear Joanna's voice echo throughout my head.

"No, No, No. Not now. This is my time. I want to experience this. Go away Joanna." I scream out into the night so loudly that I am afraid Jon hears me.

Suddenly, I stop and turn around to see if he is following me. When I don't immediately see him, I stand perfectly still and listen intently to hear him. Nothing, nothing at all except for the crickets singing and the sound of the owl as it flies in its search for its next meal.

"Shit." I cry out when I become frustrated and realize that he must be almost upon me.

I should have never stopped. Why would I do that?

"I hear you little bird. I am hungry and I want to taste the sweetness of your flesh." He says loudly before he lets out a deep howl that cuts through the night.

As soon as he says it, I turn around and realize that he must be right behind the big oak tree no more than 20 feet from me. Sure enough, he steps out into the clearing, and I see his wide eyes as he stares at me with murderous intent. A Cheshire Cat smile spreads across his lips as he lunges for me.

It is already too late, he has me backed against the next Oak tree as I feel the bark digging into my back. When he leans down and bites the side of my neck hard, I wince and close my eyes because he is a natural born killer like I am. If the shoe were on the other foot, and it was me, I would have ripped out his throat, instead of just breaking the first layer of skin.

Chapter 2: The Game Continues

As I stare up into his wild eyes, the moonlight illuminates his handsome face. I swallow hard. Probably harder than I should, because now he frowns and then all the feeling disappears from his eyes as they turn cold, dark and mirror my own soul. What I see is someone on the precipice of a never-ending battle.

"He is trying to decide if he should kill me or not?" I think to myself as I keep both eyes glued to his.

Even though I am staring into his eyes, I still watch his hands out of the corner of mine. He raises his right to my throat and starts to squeeze tight. I push myself into the bark as it bites into my skin and then just as I am about to knee him in the balls, he shakes his head and releases his grip on me, just a bit. He has absolutely no idea what I was about to do or how close he came to dealing with Joanna, when he leans his head down so his lips can devour mine hungrily.

When I relax into his arms, I remember that this is still a game, so I push past him and take off running. But not before I turn my head and stick my tongue out at him.

"Catch me if you can." I say as my taunt echoes throughout the night air.

By the time he realizes that I am still very much playing the game, I am halfway across the field before I stop, turn, and stare. He smirks at me before he yells, "Oh, I intend to. Now, little bird, I suggest you run faster than that. Or this hungry wolf will tear into that sweet little ass."

A big smile spreads across my face as I lick my lips deliberately and then take off again like a lightning bolt that strikes across the night sky. I hear him run after me while calling out sarcastically in a deeper tone of voice than usual, "I am coming for you Joanna." like a horror movie I once saw when I was a kid, and my parents were still alive.

"Not that far behind me." I think to myself as I keep running as fast as I can, but then I stop and swivel on my heels as I stare in the direction of where he should be coming from.

When I don't see him, I stop and listen. Immediately the hair on the back of my neck stands on end and I feel him, somewhere near me. Even though I don't see him, I can tell that he sees me. The predator in me tells me I know this to be the truth as I begin to run again in the same direction as I started out.

"Joanna, I am coming to get you." He taunts loudly now as if he is closer than I could have ever suspected.

This time when I stop, I crouch down in hopes that he won't see me. Too late, as I heard a twig snap to my right and look around to meet him running at me. How in the hell did he catch up with me so fast?

I stand up and bolt in the opposite direction, but not fast enough because a second later I feel his fingers wrap around my wrist tightly and yank me to him. Now, I am forced to look up into those wild, unbridled eyes and I realize something. He is laughing at me maniacally. The man I love is bat shit crazy and I thought I was the insane one.

This time when he devours my lips hungrily, I play along and let him believe I am helpless.

"Oh, poor little bird." He says softly between his urgent kisses.

Then his right-hand tangles in my locks and he pulls my head back sharply. His eyes are on the prize as he bites my neck hard and clenches his teeth on my jugular. At first, I think he is going to let go right away so I don't panic, but when he continues his relentless assault on me, I decide this is the time for it.

I start to claw at his bare forearms and dig in with my nails. Then when I feel the slick warmth of his blood on my fingertips, I look at him and notice that it isn't fazing him at all. Does this man not feel pain? I sure do, even if the rest of me feels dead.

As I try to cry out, I realize one thing. He isn't going to let go and I am going to die right here, right now as I already start to feel faint. When I continue to claw at his skin to no avail, I start to fight harder and manage to stomp on his foot. Finally, it snaps him out of whatever trance he was in for a split second, but it is long enough for me to shove him backwards, right into a medium sized spruce tree.

He shakes his head as he watches me step backwards slowly and carefully. My heart feels like it is beating out of my chest as he walks towards me quickly with a furrowed brow and then he slams me hard up against the next nearest tree. As he stares at me with hooded eyes, he bites my lower lip hard and then tugs on it while both his hands press into my sides. Then he moans when I lower my hand to his groin and tighten my grasp.

When he devours my mouth as if he owns me, I match him, and our tongues do a violent dance. My teeth gnash against his, and our nails dig each other's skin until we bleed as if we are wild animals in heat.

Then as he rips off my white, v neck T-shirt, I stare up at him fleetingly before I unzip his pants with a real sense of urgency. I need him now, as much as he needs me.

He throws his head back and emits a loud inhuman howl at the moon before his gaze returns to mine and he laces his fingers in the belt loops of my jeans. He pulls them down violently without hesitation as he licks his lips impatiently. As soon as I manage to get them off my feet, he shoves me down to my hands and knees before lining up behind me.

As I feel him thrust deep inside of me, he wastes no time and digs his fingers into my hips so he can gain leverage. I cry out in a strange sort of need and in pain at the same time because for some reason he feels bigger than he ever has before. Not to mention, he is being more forceful as he fucks me so hard that I could swear I feel him in my kidneys.

A second later, I hear him growl deeply and then he stops suddenly while he seems to be listening for something. When I look up at his face, I don't even recognize him in the dark because he looks almost animalistic with wild eyes and his stubble growing rapidly. His hair is a mess and when he stares at me, he has hunger in those eyes of his.

When he seems to be satisfied with whatever he was worried about, I feel his rock-hard shaft leave my throbbing pussy and then he rubs it on my rim slowly while he teases me with it. As he does it, I feel the heat of his stare before I feel the tip of his cock thrust in and out, just an inch. He continues to tease me by slipping in only that same inch, over and over until I clench down on it tightly.

The moment I do, he notices and then rewards me with a quick thrust of all his thick and pulsating nine inches. I cry out in need, and bite my lip before he raises his right hand and slaps my ass hard, hard enough to leave it bright red. All the while my fingers are digging into the dirt, so I don't fall forward.

I look behind me to where he is hunched over me grunting, and sweating and then I start to pant when he picks up speed. I shove my ass into him with every thrust so he gets in deeper and harder as I hear him slap up against my ass, because I can already feel myself ready to dive over the edge. But when he slides his hand down to my nub and starts to pinch it hard between his thumb and forefinger, that is it. I can't hold it any longer. As I close my eyes and see the brilliant light display, I feel him release as well, and fill my tight little ass completely.

When I begin to feel the hot seed leak down my leg, I hear him yell, "Fuck!" as he smacks my ass hard again and then leans down to place butterfly kisses on my shoulders. A few minutes later as he begins to thrust in and out again, he traces his fingers lightly down my spine and he whispers breathlessly, "Joanna, I love you. I didn't think it was possible given the fact that I have never loved anything in my life, but I do."

As soon as I hear him say it, I turn my head and look up at him before saying sarcastically, "Baby, you have the sweetest pillow talk, especially for a man who is knee deep in my ass."

Wait a minute. I didn't say that Joanna did.

Chapter 3: Jon, You Are Losing It

"Baby, what's wrong? You seem different." I ask her hesitantly, because…well she is right. I am knee deep in her ass and it feels perfect.

That nice little ass of hers is so tight and when I slide my cock in, she has this habit of making it tighter and tighter. I can't get enough. I may even like it better than her hot pussy. Honestly, I don't know if I have ever been able to say that one before.

She pauses before replying and I see a change in her face. So quickly that I could have dismissed it if she hadn't just said what she said. After all, she can be sarcastic but that sounded quite hateful.

I watch as she shakes her head slowly and then the familiar look in her eyes returns as she frowns. She looks up at me as I decide to keep going because well….I am still horny as hell. The fun we just had made the hunter in me come to the surface a little too well. As a matter of fact, for a minute there I could swear that I lost control.

"Noth…nothing is wrong. Why?" she asks wearily as she cocks her head and stares at me.

Why? Why is she scared? If I didn't have my cock in her ass, maybe I would stop to care. But right now, I just need relief because my balls are throbbing and getting hard as a rock. Not to mention, I can already tell that I will have blue balls if I don't take care of this now.

As I thrust deep inside her and feel her hot insides milk me for all my worth, I swallow hard and grunt before I begin to thrust even faster. I need to cum so hard and I need it now. So, as I switch between her slippery little ass to her wet pussy, I moan and throw my head back before I close my eyes.

"Mm. God, I love the way you feel. I love everything about you, even your little quirks." I murmur under my breath as I fill her balls deep.

As I slide in and out, I hear the sucking sounds of sex and the slapping of skin as it drives me wild. I keep thrusting in and out quickly while I smack her ass on the same spot I did before. It makes a loud crack as I feel my palm burn, then I rub her skin softly before I trail my fingers over to her rim.

Around, around, around my thumb goes as it trails in a circle around it, before I thrust it in at the same time as my cock buries itself deeper in her pussy. "You are daddy's girl. Aren't you?" I ask as I watch my thumb slide in and out of her asshole and she tightens.

As it does, I feel my heavy balls slap against her nub and a burst of pleasure follows every time it hits.

"That's my good girl!" I exclaim while I think about just how good my cock feels in any of her holes.

With my left hand, I take a fistful of silky hair and yank her head back violently, so I feel like I'm in total control. In and out, in and out, I slide my finger and then I decide to replace my thumb with the tip of my cock because I love her ass. Then I stop and revel in the feeling. It is so tight, hot and forbidden. But it feeeeels so good.

"Fuck, baby your ass is so sweet that I bet it tastes like candy." I say softly while feeling her tighten around me.

The moment I slip my shaft back in, I sense a change in her. One that is unmistakable because she turns her head and looks at me with that blank, dead stare. How could I have forgotten that she has two personalities? And how many other times has her darker side come out to play without me realizing it was her? Or am I merely going crazy? Jon, you are losing it.

"Now, does my good girl want a reward for doing such a good job?" I pause and ask before I begin to fuck her faster and faster.

Right as I plunge into her for the last time, I feel her squeeze me tight and shake. Then my hot cum spills out and fills her tight little rear. This time when I pull out, it sprays all over her ass and I begin to rub my fingers in it as I play with a smirk on my face. For some reason, I have always loved rubbing cum all over a woman's skin. Claiming her as mine. So animalistic and primal.

"Mm." I say softly as I lean over her and rub the head of my cock on her slippery ass one last time.

"That was incredible baby. You won first place. Do you want to know what the prize is?" I ask curiously while watching her face for her reaction.

She hesitates, and then looks up at me again as she digs her nails into the dirt and thrusts her ass up even higher towards my face.

"Yes. But I would love it if you licked me clean. Especially, if you use the flat of your tongue, because I love the feel of the rough side as it tickles my ass." she says in a little girl's voice while begging me at the same time with those eyes of hers.

She thrusts her butt up even further until I decide to reward her and kneel. As I bury my face in her ass, I slowly lick her clean as she asked. I can tell it does tickle her a bit because when I run the flat of my tongue over her rim, she shivers and giggles. Then I roll up my tongue and slide it in before I dig deeper.

As I thrust in and out with my tongue, I trail my fingers up her inner thigh and trace her soaked folds with my fingers. Then one by one I slip them in before I twirl them around inside. She begins to pucker her ass and clench down on my fingers as she moans loudly.

She cries out, "Jon, I need more." Before I insert all four fingers and I begin to suck her ass out.

But when I rub her clit and then slap it, she goes wild and begins to pant as she begs. Then she clenches tightly on my fingers, and I feel her ass tighten before she squirts all over my face. I was not prepared for the sheer quantity as I back up and I watch it spray outward a good 5 or 6 inches. Before this, I had never seen a woman squirt so much in my life.

When she stops a second later, I watch as she slowly pushes off the ground and turns around to stare at me in a haze. She looks tired, but then again it is early in the morning, and we have been playing for quite a while. So, I ask thoughtfully, "Are you alright?"

She nods, and then states matter-of-factly, "Of course I am. We have just had one hell of a night. Now if you don't mind, do you think you could help me find my clothes?"

I smile mischievously as I remember that I have shredded her top, but her pants are somewhere around here. As I spot them not more than 10 feet away, I point in the direction and state calmly, "Over there, but your shirt you will have to just do without. I have a blanket in the trunk you can use to wrap it around you though until we get back."

"No, no that won't do. I just know that as soon as we get back, Nick or someone will come out of their apartment and catch me wrapped in a blanket. I will never hear the end of it. That boy already wants to fuck me nonstop." she says flatly as she shakes her head in disgust.

"Well, how about this. Put your pants on and I will give you, my shirt. That way if we run into anyone, they will just see me shirtless. Is that a deal?" I ask as I watch her pick up her pants and lean up against the nearest tree to stabilize herself.

When she walks over to me, she gazes up at me with that blank stare and says flatly, "We have a deal."

As I take off my shirt and hand it to her, a satisfied smile spreads across her beautiful lips and she says seductively, "Thank you daddy."

I don't know why, but just the way she says it this time rubs me the wrong way. After all, I have never been the type of guy that got off on role playing and I only did this for her because she liked it, but. Like I said, this time it is different. There is something wrong.

I can feel it in my bones, and I don't like where this whole thing is going. Not one bit.

"Come on. Let's get going back before the sunrises and we get caught. This is not State land after all." I say softly as she follows me back through the woods and to the car.

"What do you mean?" she asks curiously as she cocks her head to stare at me once we are at the car and she looks so damn fine while wearing my shirt.

I unlock my door and then hit the button to open her side before I answer her quietly. "I found out about this place years ago when I was with this woman from an internet dating site. She had introduced me to this older man who wanted me to join in with them. Of course, at the time I had no idea that he was the one who wanted to have sex with me. But, as soon as he tried to fuck me up the ass, I left and haven't been back since. When you showed me what you like, I remembered this place and figured I would let you in on one of the things I get off on. After all, I have never had someone that I can confide in without worrying when I will have to kill them."

She shakes her head instead of saying anything as she climbs in and looks through her purse frantically.

"Where is it?" she asks fearfully when she looks up at me with a startled look in those beautiful but soulless eyes.

"What? What's wrong baby?" I ask in return because by now I am wondering what on earth could make her so scared.

Immediately she settles down and buckles in before she turns to stare out the window. As I put the key in the ignition, she says nothing, so I turn the radio on and listen to it the whole way back to her apartment while a beautiful sunrise illuminates the sky behind us in the rearview mirror.

I love this woman, but how can I tell which version of her is the right one?

Chapter 4: When The Sun Rises

"It looks like no one is up yet." I say happily as I walk up to my apartment while Jon follows behind me.

I just can't believe this shit. One minute I am having fun, and then things turn for the worse when she shows up. How did I let my guard down so much that she could easily get in?

"Most importantly, why did he look as if he wasn't too sure that he wanted to go home with me afterwards?" I ask myself as I unlock the door and open it.

Did she do or say something to scare him? Or is he getting bored with me already and wants a new plaything? After all, I am sure that his blood lust must be playing havoc with him when he couldn't satisfy his blood thirsty urges. I know that Joanna is already hungry for her next victim, and I don't know if I can hold her off for very much longer.

"Yeah, I guess we were lucky." He says absent mindedly after shutting the door behind him.

When he looks at me again, I can tell that he is not all here, and it makes me wonder what exactly his problem is.

"You know, I need to go to work today. Are you going to be staying here? Or will you decide to take off again?" he says hesitantly as he cocks his head and stares at me.

I swallow hard and then blurt out angrily for him insinuating that I can't be trusted, "You are not my keeper. I am an adult and perfectly capable of taking care of myself."

He shakes his head and then runs his right hand through his bangs before he lowers his eyes and demands, "Just stay here. The last thing I need right now is for the love of my life to go running off and screwing everyone she comes across, just to prove a point."

After he says it, he sighs and then turns to walk out. When he opens the door and leaves, panic rushes through me and I almost run after him. But I don't because I feel suffocated as Joanna takes over and I watch from the sidelines.

While I take a shower, all I can think about is the fact that I need to get Jon out of my head for good. I need to fuck someone fast and then watch as the life leaves his eyes. Not to mention I am hungry, hungrier than I have ever been in my life.

By the time I step out of the shower, I am so relaxed that I take my time and slip into the sluttiest red dress that I own. Then drive to the next town over before finding a seedy bar.

"Mm. Just perfect." I purr as I look in the rearview mirror at my reflection and pucker my blood red lips one last time.

Just as I wrap my fingers around the faux leather door handle, I notice a group of bikers hanging out by the door. With their long hair and black leather, they look threatening, but I know better because I used to have a couple of biker friends growing up. Usually, they are normal people who just like open roads. However, on closer inspection, I take that back and wonder if I should get out of the car or move on to the next bar down the road.

As I breathe deeply, I decide to chance it and open the door before standing up. But before I do, I grab my trusty knife from my purse and slip it in my matching red panties, just in case. Right away I hear one of them whistle as he stares at me lecherously.

"Oh, damn baby. Come over here and sit on my face. Once I make you cry, I will bend you over and fill that sweet little ass of yours. You won't want any other man after I am done with you." The man with the long tangled black hair and a scar that runs across his cheek says as he walks towards me quickly.

I guess I underestimate the length of his legs because before I can move out of the way, his hands are all over me. He pulls me to him and into the shadows as my adrenaline kicks in and I am ready to run at a minute's notice. However, when I watch the whole group surround me, I know I am in trouble.

"Hey, boys. Are you looking for a good time?" I say sarcastically, because if I cry out, it will only serve to fuel their hunger.

I have only been in this position once before and to my surprise it was quite pleasurable. But that night I did not get my kill as I so desired and it drove me wild. Afterwards, I ended up finding a homeless man and leading him off into the shadows so I could kill him. The problem was that I didn't have time to take care of the body as a car drove by and almost saw me. I thought for sure that was the end of it for me.

As I feel one of the other men come up behind me and his rock-hard shaft presses against my ass, the man in front of me begins to whisper, "Have you ever been gang banged baby? Because right now the boys are looking at you as if they can't wait to sink their teeth into you. And it is a shame because you are such a pretty little thing, but you won't be when they get done with you."

He runs his filthy dirty fingers over my freshly showered skin as he licks his lips and begins to smirk. Then he cups my chin and leans down to force entry into my mouth with his tongue. As soon as his other hand grabs my breast, I bite down hard on his tongue.

He steps back and spits out blood before seething, "You fucking cunt. Now we really are going to have fun with you because I like the feisty ones. Boy, oh boy, he is going to love fucking your asshole until you bleed."

I look down as he unzips his pants before he pulls it out and begins to stroke it slowly at first.

"Come on boys. It's time." He says breathlessly as he strokes himself again and nods in the direction of the back of the bar.

While two of them drag me by my arms, I kick and bite at them as I angrily state, "If anyone puts their dick in my mouth, I will bite it clean off. I don't suck cock for anyone."

As soon as I say it, the whole group laughs loudly and then we go into the shadows behind the bushes. I hear the loud rock music from the bar boom out into the morning as it masks their remarks. But when they stop and scan the area, I manage to stand, and I decide in that instant that this will work to my advantage.

Let them gang bang me all they want, but the moment they try to really hurt me, I will slice their throats and exact my revenge. So, as I watch them do a once over of the area and they let go of me briefly, I slip the knife out of my panties. Then I transfer it to the underneath of my hand where I secure it in my watch band, so it won't fall when they start to get rough with me.

"Alright, I'm first Miles." A tall man in his forties says in a raspy voice as he steps forward, and I see that he is ruggedly handsome in spite of his broken nose.

"Sure?" Miles says begrudgingly as he steps back and makes room for the taller man.

When he steps in front of me and cups the side of my cheek before he runs his thumb slowly over my lower lips, I stare at him entranced. For some reason, he has a hold over me that I simply can't break and has a presence about him that says you are mine and you will like it. However, when he slides his hands down my dress before ripping the thin fabric clean off me, I can't help but want him.

Willingly, I drop down to my knees and wait for him to do whatever he wants to me because his ice-cold blue eyes are staring down at me as they say, "You are mine."

As soon as I realize that I ache for him, a smirk plays on my lips, and I open my mouth before licking it. I watch as he unzips his pants and then pulls out the biggest dick I have ever seen in my life. If I must gamble, I must say that it is a good foot long and thick. It curves to the right and when his hand strokes it, he just rubs the tip because his hand can't fully circle it.

"Fuck, you are beautiful!" he exclaims as I watch precum form on the tip.

Not only am I hungry for him, but I feel ravenous.

"No!" I cry out unexpectedly from nowhere as I shake my head and then quickly recover.

Sure enough, she is trying her hardest to push me back down, but that little bitch won't win this time. After all, I have waited all these years for my time, and my time is now.

Chapter 5: Gang Bang

When the tall man hears me cry out "No!" He mistakes it for a challenge and decides to go ahead. So, he wanders behind me and kneels. I hear the gravel scatter as his knees hit the ground. However, I don't quite expect to feel so much pain as I do the moment, he digs his fingers into my sides and then thrusts in hard.

I feel my skin split to accommodate such a massive shaft. Then I hear him take a sharp breath in as he realizes just how tight it is. As he begins to fuck me even harder, I bite my lower lip because to scream, is to show weakness. That is something you never show to them, never. Not even if it hurts so bad that you just wish that it was anyone else but you.

"Fuck me, you are so goddamn tight." he murmurs under his breath as his fingers tear at my skin.

As he fucks me senseless, another man closes in on me and unzips his pants. He stares at me hungrily and licks his lips as a smirk plays at the corners of his mouth. Then I feel the tall man behind me who I can only think of as the leader. He stops for a second as I feel his breath on me the moment he leans down and whispers in my ear, "You bite him bitch and you die. Do you understand me?"

I turn my head to look him in the eyes before I reply sarcastically, "Yes sir. Will there be anything else?"

He spanks me hard as I feel my skin sting and I hear a loud crack, then I return my attention to the man in front of me. Right now, he is busy stroking himself slowly as he watches me intently. Then and only then, he stops and guides him into my mouth. "Filthy fucking animal." I think to myself as I close my eyes and gag when he shoves it down my throat.

Not only do I gag, but I start to feel the vomit rise in my throat as the tall man behind me groans and then empties himself in me. Slowly, one by one they take their turns fucking me in every hole as I pretend that I am enjoying myself. However, when the line is gone and they are all spent, I pretend like nothing has happened and slowly stand up to smile at them because now it is my turn.

As I straighten up, I collect what's left of my dress and then walk over to the leader before I run my finger slowly over his cock. Then I beg seductively, "Daddy, can I please have more?"

When he takes the bait and replies quietly, "Baby girl, you don't know what you do to me. To think that you want me to wreck you, makes my dick so hard it isn't funny. Now, suck me right here first to show daddy just how much his little baby girl wants him."

As soon as he says it, a Cheshire cat smile spreads across my blood smeared lips and I unzip his pants to suck him dry. I now have a sense of purpose and that is to kill this mother fucker even if it is the last thing I do.

"Oh, fucking god. Baby girl, you have the most amazing mouth." He cries out as he takes my neck in his hands and he begins to squeeze.

I stare up into his hungry eyes and hate him with all my being. For all those years I was fucked by my dad. For every single man who looked at me like a piece of meat. Then as I fill his cock swell and pulsate, I grab his balls and squeeze before I start to faint.

"Fuck me!" he exclaims as he lets go of my neck and pulls out before he punches me hard in the nose.

"So much for that." I think to myself as I hear the crunching of bone and feel a searing pain as I almost black out.

I wanted to kill him, but now I must think about the fact that if I am not careful, I won't even live long enough to exact my revenge. So, I cower as I stand and stare at him through my swelling lids before I say softly, "I like it when you're rough."

As I smile, I spit out the blood that is flowing down my throat and then I ask again, "Why don't you find us a place to be alone? I have been very bad and need a good beating, so I don't do it again."

He turns around to face me this time with a lecherous look in his eyes and he replies sarcastically, "Hm. Perhaps daddy does need a good bitch to fuck up. Come with me."

He gestures for me to follow him as he rips off his shirt and gets on his bike before he points behind him. I listen like a good little girl but am always ready to fuck his shit up at any second. Then he throws me the shirt and smiles while he watches me put it on carefully over my swollen nose and I get on behind him. As soon as I hear the engine roar to life and feel the vibration between my legs, I can understand why so many women live this life willingly. After all, it isn't always that you have almost a half-ton of vibrator between your legs.

While I can barely feel my face, I manage to laugh at the thought of it. Me on this bike, while looking like shit. It is not what I had thought would happen when I started out this morning. But it is what it is.

Not only did I get the fuck of my life, but now I get to do some truly bad things to him. I smirk as I see my reflection in the rearview mirror and realize that I only have his shirt on and my torn panties. When I look down at my watch, I smile again because the knife is still there, barely, but it is and that is all that counts because I will be needing it soon enough.

About a half an hour later, he stops at a motel down on route 129 and gets us a room for the night. Then he sees the restaurant next door and casually asks about it before he turns to me and winces when he realizes how bad my face must hurt.

"Come on. Let's go." He says absent mindedly as he stares at the young man behind the counter with curly red hair and the greenest eyes.

As I follow him to room 3 right by the office, I notice that there is no one else in the parking lot. Perhaps, the young man is not as stupid as he acts, because this way he can keep an eye on us. Especially when as we walked out the door, I watched him pick up the phone and call 911. However, that means I don't have much time before I need to disappear, so I must work fast.

The moment he shuts the door and turns around, I smile seductively and pull my shirt off so I can draw him in close. Then when he says softly, "Oh, baby girl I love those titties of yours." I decide to strike.

As I slip the knife from under my watch band, I stick him like a pig in his belly and slice it right across from side to side. His intestines spill out, but not before I quickly bring my blade to his throat and make my cut. It stops him from saying a word, and the moment I do, I start to laugh.

It is an uncontrollable laugh as if I had just finally completely lost my mind. But as I stand there laughing, I still remember to cut off his ear as he lay on the floor with blood spraying out all over.

"Wow. What a mess!" I exclaim as it gets all over my shoes.

"I guess it is a good thing that I wore red shoes today, isn't it?" I say jokingly before I bend down and slice the earlobe clear off.

Now I can make my escape before the cops get here and I am thrown in jail. But when I hear the siren of a squad car pulling in, I begin to panic. I look around quickly to find another way to escape and as I rush into the bathroom, I see a small window above the toilet.

I quickly slide it sideways and then push the screen out before I slip out and into the alley behind the motel. Luckily, they have not thought about surrounding the place, so I manage to hide under the cover of the bushes until I am far enough away that I begin to walk in the shadows.

Chapter 6: Beggars Can't Be Choosy

When I come upon a little one story, grey house with a white picket fence, I see several items of women's clothing hanging up in the yard. After I stop and quickly take them before anyone notices me, I hunch down in the brush to change before I realize that it won't matter anyways. My face will cause anyone to stop and ask questions.

"Damn it!" I exclaim when I run my first finger down the line of my nose.

It not only hurts, but I can already tell that it is crooked. "That will make it that much harder to get my prey in the future." I murmur under my breath as I stand up and admire my handiwork.

The faded blue jeans are a little too big and the red patchwork top is a bit too small, but it will just have to work. After all, "beggars can't be choosy." My mom would always say when I would turn my nose up to a vegetable I didn't like.

The minute my dad would come home from work I always hid behind her long flowery skirts, because I never liked the way he looked at me with that crooked smile and those promising eyes. Especially after I found out what he was promising late at night, when the moon was full, and the stars were bright. The funniest part of it all was that while I tried not to concentrate on what he was doing, the scars on his body would always make me wonder where he got them from. But I didn't dare ask, never.

An hour or so after I begin walking down the road, I manage to flag down someone to take me back to the bar. After all, I figure by now that they would have all moved on. Probably in hopes of catching up with their leader. But little do they know that he won't ever be riding anything again, let alone his motorcycle.

As I think about it, I giggle and stare out the window while rubbing the earlobe in my pants pocket. When I do, the man next to me, places his hand on my inner thigh and glances over at me hungrily. A second later, I lick my lips and ask seductively, "Do you want to fuck?"

He breathes in deeply and then pulls over along the side of the deserted road. At first, I didn't want to do it because he seemed halfway decent until this moment. Although, there is the fact that he has a wedding ring on, and he had just showed me the picture of his kid's smiling face after I agreed to climb in. That is definitely not working in his favor.

When I decide to do this, I turn to stare him point blank in the eyes before I say sarcastically, "Well fuck Chuck. I thought you were a family man, and you were different than all the rest. But it just goes to show that every single man in existence thinks only with his dick."

"Now, now don't be such a big bitch." He replies spitefully as he slides his fingers up to my center and begins to rub my clit through the fabric.

I hear a click as he presses the lock button on his side, so I start to laugh maniacally while I swat his hand away and state flatly, "Don't you ever fucking dare touch me again. If you know what is best for you, you will unlock this door right now and let me out."

He leans over to practically spit in my face as he stares me down and replies, "Oh, really. And just what will you do if I don't because I have half a mind to just fuck you right now anyways. I would love to bend you over in the backseat and christen that beautiful asshole of yours like I did my wife's."

As he says it, he stops and stares at me then he smirks and adds snidely, "Or have you already been fucked up the ass? I bet you're a dirty girl and you love it that way. Don't you?"

I humor him because this game has suddenly gotten interesting as I ask mockingly, "Don't you?"

"What do you mean?" he asks hesitantly as he cocks his head and stares at me intently.

I swallow before I clear my throat and ask sarcastically with a serious face, "Don't you like to be fucked up the ass? You look like the type that would."

He coughs and then replies angrily, "Look bitch. I don't know what the fuck your problem is, but I am neither gay nor any weird shit like that. What I am is horny as fuck, so get to it."

As he points down to his package with both his hands, he looks at me impatiently. But when I refuse to move, he reaches over and grabs a fistful of my hair before he yanks me towards him. "Not now, not ever." I state quickly as I withdraw the knife from my pocket and in one fluid movement, I slice his throat open.

Blood begins to spray everywhere, but I don't care as I reach over him and hit the unlock button calmly. Then I scan the area before I open the door. No more than two minutes later, I walk away as if nothing had just happened, even though I have blood on my face, and it is staining the freshly laundered shirt that I am wearing.

"What a pity." I state as I shake my head and look around for another outfit to wear.

It does not take me too long to find a long black dress hanging on a clothesline behind a little run-down shack. I could swear that luck is working for me today when I notice that it fits me exactly right. Not only does it accentuate my curves, but it is the only color that truly looks good on me. Black.

Now, before you go saying that black is not a color, remember from art class when they taught you that black is a mixture of all the colors. White is the absence of them and anything in between is just plainly a color, nothing else. I always fought with my teacher and told her that no one really cares about if black is a color or not. For that, I got sent to the principal's office every time.

Chapter 7: Just Walk Away

"Jon, Jon, Jon. You never learn. You should just walk away from her now before you can't anymore." I murmur under my breath before I sigh and wait in my car.

Of course, by the time I returned from the precinct, she was gone. I really should have known, but I had thought she learned after the last time. God, I was so fucking wrong that it hurts right down to my toes.

It isn't even the fact that she lied to me that concerns me, but that she hurts herself when she does this. And I am beginning to wonder if she hasn't lost herself to her darker side. After all, she seems different, wrong somehow.

If I could put a nail in it, I would say that she is a different person entirely than the woman I fell in love with. But is she, or am I just kidding myself? Because if her other side has taken over finally, what will I do about it? Or more aptly put, what can I do about it?

A few minutes later, I start to slouch down in the seat when I watch her drive up in her car. As she passes me, she doesn't even seem to notice me sitting here because she is facing away from me. On further inspection, she looks as if she is drunk or drugged up in a weird sort of way as she staggers towards the door. Eventually, I decide that maybe I had better just go back to my place and think about it for a while.

So, I put the key in the ignition and twist it. The engine roars to life and as I back up, I watch her walk into the apartment building all by herself. She has a weird long dress on that I have never seen before that looks so out of place on her it isn't funny. Even though I know better, I continue to back up. I don't look back, even when that voice in my head tells me to go to her.

"No, damn it. If she really wanted me, she wouldn't have left and listened to me for once. Of course, she didn't. So, fuck her and the horse she rode in on.

After I drive home, I sigh and then turn the car off before I go inside. It has been at least a week since I have been home. I am just glad that I don't have a pet because it would have been dead by now.

I laugh when I walk into the kitchen and open the fridge to find a loaf of moldy bread. As I turn around, I notice that there are flies surrounding the trash can. When I look in it, I see maggots crawling up the sides.

"Shit. Now that is gross." I cry out as I see a half-eaten piece of lasagna in the bottom that is infested with them.

They are literally making it look alive as the sides swell with their every movement. "God how gross is that?" I think to myself as I quickly tie off the bag and take it out to the curb.

I swallow hard after I wash my hands and decide that this just won't do. How could I have left everything go so long without ever thinking about it? Because of her, that's how.

As I picture Joanna in my mind, one thing is clear. I can't live without her. But can she live without me?

When I finally sit down in my leather reclining chair a few minutes later, I close my eyes and realize that she obviously can.

"Now what?" I say to an empty room as I don't know what to do with myself.

Nothing feels right without Joanna. Nothing at all. Yet a few minutes later that hunger returns. That familiar call of the blood, and that gives me an idea, so I pull out my phone and look in the newspaper app for anyone who has been accused of child abuse but got out on bond.

When I find a winner, I smile from ear to ear and prepare myself for the hunt by showering and shaving. Then I make sure that I put on my leather gloves that are thick enough to not leave fingerprints. Before I get in the car and swing by Mr. Caterra's house on 7th street.

As it just so happens, he is coming home, and he has his young son with him. "Bingo."

I watch as he drags him in the house by his ear and I can already tell by the bruises on his arms that he has taken a beating by this man.

"You will pay for what you did." I murmur under my breath before I get out of the car with my blade in one hand behind my back.

As I approach the house, I hear the poor kid crying as his dad swears at the top of his lungs, "You shithead. I will make sure you never do that again. Get down on your knees so I can show you what it means to pray."

The moment I hear that, I open the front door and surprise spreads across his face.

"Who the fuck are you?" He yells angrily as his fists come up to punch me in the face.

I dodge quickly and then I pull the cold steel from behind my back as I stab him right in the heart. After all, there is no need to necessarily scar the kid for life by butchering him right in front of the son.

Instead, I yell at him to go to his bedroom as I prepare myself to do what I do. So, after I make sure that the kids bedroom door is shut, I wrap the dad up in the living room rug before I carry him out to the car. I open the trunk and quickly put him in before anyone gets the chance to see me. Then I go back in to make sure the kid says nothing to anyone.

When I open his door, he looks down and he sees all the blood covering my hands, so I drop to my knees and I say softly, "You will never have to worry again if he will beat you, but I need to be able to trust you. You won't say anything about this will you?"

He nods slowly and then leans forward to give me a big hug. He whispers, "Thank you." And then he runs over to his bed and hides his face in the pillow. I know that he is crying, but that is alright now. Everything will be from now on.

Or will it? Because after I dispose of the body, I know what I must do, and it won't be easy. Especially when I love her so damn much.

Chapter 8: It's Just Not Meant To Be

When I wake up the next morning, I already sense that things are different. As I stretch, I love the feel of my body and the power that surges through me as I remember the way I killed those men. Not to mention, how good the warmth of their blood felt on my skin as it caressed me in ways no lover ever could.

As I revel in the memory, I smile and climb out of bed before I look in the mirror at my beautiful body even though it is torn and bruised. However, when I look up at my face, I wince because I look like someone else, but somehow it fits me now. After all, I am someone new. Someone better. I am Joanna more than I have ever been before.

"Damn girl. No wonder why every man on this planet wants to fuck you." I say to myself in the mirror as I admire myself and run my hands down my sleek body to my belly.

"It is a shame." I murmur under my breath as I wonder what it would have been like to have kids.

But then I remember exactly who and what I am before I shrug and walk over to my phone to see if Jon has called. When I see that he hasn't even texted, I cock my head and ask softly, "I wonder what the fuck is wrong with him?"

A second later when my phone rings, I almost drop it on the floor as Jon's name shows up in the contacts. In a way it scares me, but I could swear someone is telling me something. Who knows, maybe we are fated or some such bull shit like that?

When it keeps ringing, I quickly hit the answer button and hesitate before asking, "Where are you?"

There is silence on the line before I hear an echo in the phone as his heavy breathing gets louder and he finally replies in a whisper, "I am behind you."

It takes me precisely a second to turn around and hit him in the face as he scares the shit out of me. I don't like people walking up on me like that. As a matter of fact, he is just lucky that I didn't have a knife in my hand, or I would have stabbed him with it.

"What the fuck Jon?" I yell in his face while furrowing my brow and shoving him backwards with both hands.

He wraps his fingers around my wrists and pulls me to him before he says excitedly, "I feel much better now because I killed that fucker."

I cock my head and look at him curiously before I ask, "What fucker?"

He smiles so handsomely that I can't help myself when I reach over and kiss him full on the lips. However, a second later he breaks it and looks at me funny before he states coldly, "Seriously, we need to talk."

The moment I hear those words, it hits me that he is kicking me to the curb. How could he? I should be the one ditching his sorry ass, but instead I am facing a broken heart and all because I decided to be the one for once. "What the fuck?" I think to myself just when I finally win.

I follow him to the couch and then we both sit down before he furrows his brow and frowns. When he finally looks into my eyes, I know exactly what he is going to say. As he opens his mouth, I put my finger to his lips and interrupt him by saying quickly, "Don't. Just don't alright?

Let's not say it because my heart can't handle it. Not now, not ever. Especially when I didn't even think I could care about someone, let alone love someone. So, why don't you just go fuck off!" I yell at the top of my lungs and bolt straight up to a standing position.

When he follows me, he backs up with his hands in the air and replies so sadly, "Alright, I will go. I get it. I really do. Just know that I will always love you no matter what. We just can't be together without getting caught. If I ever see you again, just know that you will always be in my heart."

He turns away and then faces me one last time to kiss me sweetly on the lips before he walks to the door and states flatly, "By the way, I hope by saying this it makes this a little easier. I am a detective, and I was put on the case to catch you." He pauses before adding hesitantly, "They are hot on your tail so don't do anything stupid to get caught." Before he walks out the door slowly and never looks back.

After waking up in a cold sweat, I struggle to open my eyes because I feel like I have just run a marathon. I sigh and then raise my hand to wipe the crusts off my eyelids for merely a second, before I drop my left hand to the bed beside me. The moment I do, I notice that the black silky sheets under my fingertips seem to be wet with something warm, so I glance down. When I see it, I stare blankly at the dark red puddle staining the fabric. However, when I move my hand to the side quickly, I feel an object squish underneath the sheet.

Right away, I wonder how I could have been so stupid while climbing out of bed as quickly as I can. In the meantime, I almost trip while wiping my hand on my red silky nightgown in disgust. After all, it is stained with the same dark red substance, and I already know what has happened. The exact same thing that happens every time.

As I slide across a slippery spot on the hard-wood floor, a brief memory of last night flashes through my head before I fall on my ass in a puddle remarkably of still warm blood. "Damn it, I sure am making a fucking mess of this all." I think to myself before I push off the floor and head to the bathroom.

After fetching a few towels, I wipe up what I can of the blood before it gets in the creases of the wood planks, then I hurry to wrap up the body in the sheets. I do what I can before I hear a quick knock at the door. "Knock, knock." It comes again as I scan the room for some way to hide the evidence from the hallway.

"Knock, knock." Someone knocks several more times and louder as if they are in a hurry.

Knowing that if I open the door in my current state I will be hauled away by the cops, I stand perfectly still and hope that they just go away. However, a second later, the knocking continues. This time it is proceeded by a man's familiar deep voice stating urgently, "Open up. I know you are in there. I saw you go in with an older man."

While frantically scanning the room for a means of escape, I see the black curtains move as the breeze brushes them. Swallowing hard, I make a mad dash for the window before I hear a key in the lock and then the brass knob begins to turn slowly. I open the window the rest of the way and feel the wood under my fingers as I jump out before I even look to see what floor I am on.

Too late do I realize that I am on the second floor as I swallow hard and hope that I don't land too hard. Luckily, on my way down, a big lilac bush breaks my fall and I manage to escape with minimal cuts and bruises as I roll the rest of the way before landing on my feet, just as cats do.

As I hear someone yelling my name in the distance repeatedly, I run the opposite way and into the darkness. And when I find a big green dumpster just outside the back of the hotel, I climb inside quickly and close my eyes while I listen for anyone approaching. At first, I hear nothing, but as soon as someone finds the dead body, I begin to hear sirens surrounding the property in no time flat.

For the moment I stay put while I swallow hard and pray, because all I can do is hope that it dies down somewhat soon. After about a half hour of breathing through my mouth and sitting on the cold metal of the dumpster floor, I peek out a small crack in the lid. I see no movement, so I decide to make my move before someone finds me. After all, I need to get as far away from here as possible before the cop's corner off the area. Because once they do that, I will be trapped with no way out.

Unfortunately, while climbing out of the dumpster, I hear a noise behind me and then a flash of light as a cop car drives by slowly with its lights on bright. Wishing that I had waited just a few minutes longer, I shake my head, because I am about to get caught tonight. Of course, there is always a chance they won't see me.

"Yeah right." I murmur under my breath as I hunch down perfectly still and wait.

As soon as the cop car stops, I bolt for the refuge of the darkness and hope they don't trail after me. Of course, they always do, and this is when I hear that same deep familiar voice yelling hoarsely, "It wasn't her. I know that one. We have someone in custody already."

I feel the impulse to look, but the moment I turn to glance at him, all I see is his back. By the looks of it, he has let his hair grow out and hasn't been taking care of himself like he should have. But then again, I am not there to tell him differently. I also notice that his voice sounds dry as if he has been drinking again, and he seems to be struggling to keep upright. Not the same man I once knew. Of course, did I ever really know him?

    The End

I hope you enjoyed The Bad Behavior Series. The Prequel series will be coming out within the next month or two called The Skeletons in the Closet Series. It follows Jon before he meets Joanna and their beautiful duet blossoms. Thank you for taking the time to read my books.

To my loving husband, mom, sister and all my family that believed in me enough to push me to make this all possible. Thank you. I love you all.

About the Author

M.D. LaBelle is an award-winning, international bestselling author. The genres include horror, erotica, fantasy, romance, thriller, and children's books. She lives in Michigan with her loving husband and four of their six children. Most recently she has started writing on over 200 paid web novel platforms and selling her novels on Amazon, Chapters Indigo, Barnes & Nobles, Kobo, Apple iBooks, Google Play Books and many more. Please feel free to visit her website, Instagram, Twitter and Facebook. Visit M.D. LaBelle's website at

www.mdlabelle.com

Instagram Account

www.instagram.com/M.D.LaBelle/

Twitter Account

www.twitter.com/MDLaBelle1

Facebook Account

www.facebook.com/profile.php?id=100062142582314

I hope you enjoyed reading Love Me Forever. Please take the time to read all my other novels if you haven't already and wait for the prequel series to come out within the next month or two. Thank you.

Review it. Please review this novel and let others know what you liked about this book. If you write a review, please send an email to me at m.d.labelle0@gmail.com afterwards. Or if you want, please visit me at www.mdlabelle.com

Love Me Forever

Book Three Of The Bad Behavior Series

Copyright © 2023 M.D. LaBelle

Casper Publishing

All Rights Reserved

This book is a work of fiction. Characters and names are of the author's imagination or are used fictitiously. Any resemblance to an actual person, living or dead, is entirely coincidental.

All rights are reserved. No part of this publication may be reproduced, distributed, or transmitted in any form or by any means, including photocopying, recording, or other electronic or mechanical methods, without the express prior written permission of the publisher, except in the case of brief quotations embodied in critical reviews and certain other noncommercial uses permitted by copyright law. For permission requests, please contact the author through her website: www.mdlabelle.com

www.ingramcontent.com/pod-product-compliance
Lightning Source LLC
LaVergne TN
LVHW010428070526
838199LV00066B/5965